BROKEN

But Not

DESTROYED

Pamela Ruchon

Broken But Not Destroyed

Copyright © 2023 by Pamela Ruchon

To order additional copies of this book, please contact:

MAPLE LEAF PUBLISHING INC.
www.mapleleafpublishinginc. com

General Inquiries & Customer Service
Phone: 1-(403)-356-0255

Email: info@mapleleafpublishinginc.com

ISBN Paperback: 978-1-77419-197-2
ISBN eBook: 978-1-77419-196-5

Contents

CHAPTER ONE......................... 1

CHAPTER TWO 3

CHAPTER THREE 8

CHAPTER FOUR....................... 12

CHAPTER FIVE 14

CHAPTER SIX......................... 16

CHAPTER SEVEN 19

CHAPTER EIGHT 22

CHAPTER NINE 28

CHAPTER TEN......................... 32

CHAPTER ELEVEN 37

CHAPTER TWELVE................... 45

DEDICATION

*In loving memories of my grandmothers, Pinkey Gray and Alice Parquette.
Your words of wisdom, with your loving direction and correction.
Has truly enable me to stand and trust in God.
Thanks for praying me.*

CHAPTER ONE

It Begins

As she walked to her car memories burst through the corridors of her mind, like an overflowing damn.

This time I won't hold back anything, I'll tell all my secrets. Oh Lord I need to be free from all this baggage I have carried for so long. I can't change the past, but I refuse to allow the past to dictate my future.

It's three o'clock and I have to get to the club. Tonight I have to make all final arrangements, it's the Uptown Queens annual ball. I love the Second Line events, I get a theme and do my thang. Mademoiselle you would be so proud of your Honey Love. Thinking back on how she got her name Honey Love Parquette. Daddy named me Honey, he said I was the sweetest thing in the world. My Momma called me Love. She said love will always be with me, but she was wrong. Parquette because that is who I am a Parquette, strong, capable, and unbreakable.

Upon arriving at the club Ms. Ella met her at the door. Now Ms. Ella was her Godmother, hostess, manager, accountant and the overseer of all that had to do with her. Child where you been? I tried calling you after prayer meeting. We had a time (she chuckled). What's wrong Honey? Oh nothing Ms. Ella, thinking about this menu for the Queens. I know you girl that ain't nothing to think about.

You cook with your eyes close; the good Lord gave you a gift.

When it comes to feedn His People you feed the body and the soul. Speaking of the soul I know you got a wonderful message for Sunday. Tears begin to roll down her face.

Ms. Ella Sunday will be the seventh anniversary of Joshua's abduction. With her arms holding her tight Ms. Ella said "Baby I see your pain and God feels your hurt". It's sad and terrible but look how the Lord has used you. So many families who share your pain and lost find comfort in a tragedy that yall share. Now go in that kitchen and do what you do. He got you Honey Love lets wipe those tears away. I love you Ms. Ella. Love you to Honey.

Here comes Leslie, go over everything with her. She will be finalizing everything today. Ok remember trouble don't last always. As she entered into the kitchen every thought memory hurt and pain seemed to disappear. It was the one place in the world where she was in control.

Growing up after school she spent most of her time in the kitchen with Mademoiselle. It was all about creating something special outta something simple. She would say, "Honey Love life sometimes starts off with things that aren't all that great. But when you began to add the better things like a lil honey and a lotta love, you have something that's wonderful and never forgotten. Like you Honey Love. I miss my Granma so much.

CHAPTER TWO

Watching the sun creep through the long night of darkness, wondering how she would survive this day. Wiping the tears away as she looked at the picture of her forever baby Joshua. Reminiscing on the joy that he brought to her in the short time of his life. A praise began to swell in her, and the tears of a broken heart quickly turned into tears of joy. Joy simply because it don't hurt like it used to.

The doorbell ranged. Good morning Cousin. Good morning Cousin. Good morning Pastor Parquette. Good morning Deaconess Brown. They laughed, are you ok Cousin? Yes Gwen. You know it's been seven years, but God got me. This Sunday is the largest support gathering we've ever had. We got this. I'm proud of you Honey.

Get ready I know you got a Word from on high today! Yes, I do! I'll get your things together while you get ready to win this battle today. Thanks Cousin you have always been here for me, I love you. Love you to Honey Love.

Approaching True Salvation Non-Denominational Church, Honey's eyes danced with joy. Her spirit within leaped with an excitement. The parking lot was full. The neighborhood extended their driveways and even offered garage parking. One block was set up with tables, chairs and a buffet table that was nothing but mouthwatering. With buggy rides and a merry-go-round for the children. And for entertainment none other than the Make You Buck Brass Band.

Good morning Mr. Henry how you doing? Good morning Pastor Parquette. Oh, oh look around Ms. Honey see all the good Lord let me do. I'm good child, yo Grandma ah be proud of you. Well I ain't gon hold you up dem church folks waitn on you. One day Mr. Henry the Holy Ghost is going to escort you right on into your seat. Huh you know you can't see the Holy Ghost He ah ghost. Yes, Sir ok Mr. Henry.

Gwen find Red tell her to make me a plate I want the whole buffet and double dessert. Ok I'll see you inside. Good morning Deaconess Cortez. Good morning Deaconess Brown. How is she Gwen?

You know Honey Love I can't tell. Yeah, she could always hide behind that big ole smile. Be praying Red. Gwen, we got her you know we already for today. Girl pray is what we do.

And speaking at the same time "And it do what it do" amen and amen.

Good morning First Lady. Good morning Honey Love. God got you now breathe. Yes Ma'am. Your ready for this day. Trust what is in you and you will be just fine. Let's walk Mr. Henry out did his self. Do you think he will ever come in? Some people are wounded so deep from church hurt they won't have nothing to do with church folks. Henry Gray is one that man got a whole lotta Word in him. Good morning First Lady. Good morning Gwen. You always look so beautiful First. Thank you, Daughter. Now I'll talk to you ladies after service.

Gwen did you get the balloons. Yes and Ms. Ella has the coupons for dinner at The Doors of Grace. We have everything under control lil cousin. Breathe Honey you can do this. God got me. Yes, He got you. Inhaling slowly and releasing the anxiety she smiled with a nod. What will I do without you Gwen? That's something we will never know.

Good morning Bishop Moore. Hello Daughter. I'm praying for you just let the Holy Spirt have His way. Yes Sir. The Lord has done just what He said He would do with your tragedy. Let those tears be tears of joy for you have overcame so many things. And now take a deep breath. Yes Sir. Bishop Moore smiled while nodding with approval.

Walking to the sanctuary everyone and everything was in place. There were chairs in the aisles, the overflow was filled to capacity. The Ushers are in position looking like soldiers. I can hear the sound of the choir robes as they enter in bringing the spirit of praise with them.

As she looked around, she could see the ones that were there for the first time. It's the blankness that's in the eyes, she knew ole so well. A body without a soul, going thru the motions and yet so detached. Praying silently, Lord Jesus you are what they need, what we have come for. Let me be your eyes, your voice, your hands. Let your love flow thru me. She than took her seat on the front row.

By this time the organ player was in a trance playing like never before. Each musician followed with a sound that made the chandeliers swing. Men are running around the church with hands up. Sisters are knelled and prostrated. They falling out right and left the glory of the Lord had entered. After the fifth selection from the choir the people was ready for the Word.

First Lady Moore approached the pulpit, with a glow of pure joy on her face. She stood with hands in the air waiting for the calm and then the stillness. As the congregation returned to their seats she began to hum. She had so much to be thankful for.

She and Mademoiselle grew up in Mississippi. And like runaway slaves they ran far from Mississippi. Living next door to each other they became more sisters as than friends. They were warned not to get close to the woods. A young girl by herself would be raped or probably murdered.

Dalilah was coming home from work at Miss Minnie's.

She was snatched by two men who intended to destroy her. Mademoiselle knew something was wrong. She went looking for her. And she found her being violated in the worst way. They say they didn't remember much except they left two white men dead in the woods. Story goes they ran and ran until the got to Nu Awlins.

Together they opened a boarding home, mostly seamen when they ships came to the port. She and Mademoiselle opened a dress shop. Dalilah Rich, a woman who did eight years in prison for possession of heroin. She came out met and married Bishop Rico Moore. They later opened a music school. From inmate to First Lady

Dalilah Moore of the True Salvation Non-Denomination Church.

After the fifth selection of the choir, the people were ready. They had danced, shouted, ran around and bowed down, they were ready. Now with interrupted thoughts of days long gone trading places with accolades. And with no further delay I present to you Pastor Honey Love Parquette.

Taking a deep breath as she entered the pulpit, she gave acknowledgments.

I want to tell you a story. A story about a man who was asked to sacrifice his son. This man was Abraham the father of faith. A man that believed God to the point where he prepared an offering to sacrifice. He understood that his son was a gift, a promise fulfilled. Looking around the room she could see tears falling from the eyes of those that had lost children. As I come to a close, I can truly say I feel your pain. I know your hurt because like you I lost my son. A son who became a sacrifice to bring us together and share with those who understands the loss. The next time you ask why, remember today. Remember Joshua and all the children we represent today.

As Honey was taking her seat, she felt a warmth in her heart. The coldness that had been there for so long had melted away. The choir sang their last selection before the benediction.

Bishop Moore dismissed the congregation, and everyone headed to the fellowship hall. Many of the people stopped Honey and thanked her for her courage and strength. They expressed their gratitude in knowing they wasn't alone.

Standing at the door was Bishop and First Lady greeting everyone. When Honey entered the foyer where they stood, she could see the joy and pride on their faces. First Lady Moore hugged her with tears in her eyes said, "Mademoiselle would be so proud of you". You did good Honey Love. In a whisper she responded thank you Teedy.

A deep voice interrupted the moment and said "You will be all right child". God is using you in a special way. Look around the joy and peace these souls have this moment. Now go get you something to eat. Yes Sir.

As usual Gwen was at the bottom of the stairs waiting to give Honey her summary of the service. Wow Cousin you preached me to a cloud somewhere up there in the sky. This is one day that will be remembered and talked about. Next year we will have to have this service at another location. You know we had overflow in the overflow. She smiled glory to the Master. Yes indeed.

I'm going to get my dinner and go home I have a long day tomorrow. Ok what time should I be ready? Get some rest tomorrow. Where are you going Honey? I'll tell you later. All right get some rest. Bye.

CHAPTER THREE

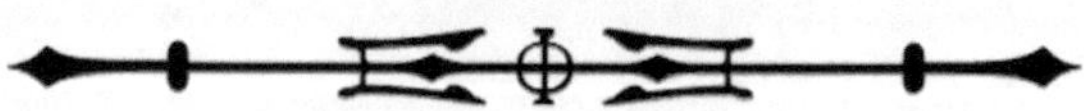

The Ride to Pickaloo

The drive was more scenic than usual. Strawberry stands are everywhere. It's that season the berries are so ripe you can smell them in the air. Wondering what secret would be revealed the ride was quiet at times not even a thought just quiet.

Today is the day that will be the beginning and the end of so much. I hope Dr. Chester is as good as they say. And maybe my mind can finally have the peace I preach about. Driving across the lake brought back fond memories of times with Daddy.

As the destination drew near Honey wondered where to start. Wondered if she really wanted to wake the demons that had directed so many events in her life.

Good morning I'm Ms. Parquette I have a ten o'clock with Dr. Chester. Yes good morning Ms. Parquette would you care for some tea or coffee? No thanks. Please take a seat. Taking her seat she wondered if the doctors were right prescribing medications for life. Hell no! I'll be all right just sometimes my head get so full. And the sadness no one knows about. I just have to let it all out and take the meds for a while and I'll be all right.

Ms. Parquette this way please. Walking down what seemed to be a very long hallway her heart begin to pound. What am I going to say? Where do I begin? Good morning Ms. Parquette. Good morning Doctor. Please have a seat. As she looked around the office it was cozy it felt safe. How are you feeling? Well I plan to make you the last psychiatrist I will ever see, so I'm going to get all my lil secrets out. Very well what are your secrets? And as though waiting for a movie to begin he sat back in his oversized chair.

Where would you like to begin? At the beginning. Okay. When I was seven Mademoiselle my grandmother took me to Chicago. It was the first time I rode the train I was so excited. The train was full of colored people all dressed up. But what I remember the most was the pink greasy chicken boxes. Everyone was smiling and so very friendly. But as the train begin to leave the station something in me became afraid. Afraid of what? I don't know but it was a bad feeling that turned out to be a real nightmare.

Gazing out of the window her thoughts took her to a place in time. An awful place a place a little girl should never go. Are you all right Ms. Parquette? After a time of silence she said it just that I've tried so hard to forget so much. Sometimes my mind feels as though its going to explode like right now! Breathe Ms. Parquette. I have to get this out.

We stayed with Mademoiselles aunt who was five years older than she was. Auntie Geneva was very beautiful. I remember her long golden hair, brown eyes and the champagne gold tooth on the side. I felt the love from her the moment she laid eyes on me. Honey Love I'm so pleased to meet you. And just then the anxiety that rode that train with me was gone.

My third day there her daughter Emma and I went to the park. Emma's boyfriend Frankie was waiting for her. At the entrance there was an old man sitting propped up against the wall. He looked like a bum but he was the devil himself. We were the only ones in the park. Emma pushed me on the swing for a while then she went a distance to make out with Frankie. The next thing I knew the old man that appeared to be passed out suddenly came alive. He covered my mouth with one dirty hand and snatched me off the swing with the other.

I became paralyzed with fear. It was the day I lost my voice…I lost a part of me. In a blink of an eye I was wrapped in the arms of all that was evil. Standing and pacing back and forth. Her heart was pounding sweat begin to bead on her forehead.

Dr. Chester looked on watching a strong confident woman

transform into a terrified little girl. But Honey mind was made up she would face this demon. He took me into a tunnel and everything was happening so fast and yet in slow motion.

It was the first time I'd ever seen a man private part. I couldn't scream couldn't speak. Not only had he taken me but he took my scream. He began to rip my clothes off while rubbing his self on my face. In seconds there I was buck naked as a new born baby. I closed my eyes and began to pray. God please come get me. Please don't let the Boogie Man hurt me. Lord I want my clothes on. Please help me. I could feel his hot sticky wet hands on my body. I tried to scream but I couldn't. And far away I could hear my name being called. I knew God heard me and was coming to get me. It was Frankie and Emma.

As the voices got closer that hard nasty thing I felt on my face. That thing that tried to invade my person was now soft and sticky. I could hear feet running. I opened my eyes and looked into the blackest nothing. He had a grip on my throat and it became harder and harder to breathe.

Frankie was getting closer calling my name. Honey Love, Honey Love. And like a ball he threw me and I hit ah wall.

When I woke up Mademoiselle was sitting next to me, on the side of the bed. I held her so tight. I wanted to tell her what that man did to me. But I couldn't speak. She said Honey we going home tomorrow. And everything will be just fine. But it wasn't.

I remember the train ride home. All I could hear was the sound of the train on the tracks. And Mademoiselle smiling holding my hand saying I love you Honey Love Parquette. I watched as she tried to hold back the tears. I could see the regret of bringing me to Chicago. The hatred for Emma leaving me alone and not watching me. The confusion as to when will I speak again. As she tried to assure me how things will be all right when we get home. The sound of the train slowly traded places with her words.

As Dr. Chester slowly rose from his chair he watched her curl into a ball of utter torment. He carefully approached her with much caution, quietly speaking her name Ms. Parquette your safe its over. With nothing but a still silence it was as though she had stopped breathing. In a soft voice he spoke her name Honey Love. Slowing raising her head as her body began to uncurl from the ball in which she found a place of safety.

Both sitting on the floor, she sighed with relief. Finally I told what happened for the first time. As Dr. Chester helped her from the floor she whispered that felt good to loose that demon. Dr. Chester that day was the beginning of so much stolen from my life. That man took my scream. You know Doc I didn't speak for three years after that day in the tunnel. He took my scream I need to scream again. Ms. Parquette you screamed today, and now your free. Free to scream to laugh you have your voice. Thank God, thank you Lord. It's over and yet it's just beginning. Ok Doc I have to leave now. I'm going to give you something to stabilize your moods. I would like to see you once a week. That's fine see you next week.

I'm going to give you something to help you with the depression. No I'm not depressed. The secrets you have carried is causing the heaviness, you hide so very well. And also something for the anxiety. I would like to see you once a week. Yes next week.

Walking to her car she stopped and began to pant as if in labor ready to deliver. Then all of a sudden a scream from the depths of her soul rang out. I screamed! OH GOD! Then another one. Oh God you gave it back. Scream after scream its been thirty years thank you Lord!

People were looking and some even rushed to help. As she begin to compose herself she could see the confusion on the faces of those that came to her aide. Looking around at the confused faces she saw only one face that understood. After receiving a nod of approval from Dr. Chester all she could do was lift her hands in praise.

CHAPTER FOUR

Back at The Club

As Honey was getting ready for the Uptown Queens Court announcement the phone ranged. Hello. Hey Honey. Hey Gwen. Are you ready? I'm on my way to the club. I'm just putting this hat together. You know I have to look as good as my food look and taste. They laughed. All right I'll meet you there.

Cousin I want you to hear something first. She let out a scream that sounded like an alarm. Gwen begin to cry and praise God. Wait, wait, wait. Oooeee Honey how? When did it come back? O thank you Jesus! Wait wait, wait Cousin let me catch my breath. How Honey? Yesterday Gwen I went to Pickaloo and came back with my scream.

Honey Love I am so happy for you. God said he will restore. And after all this time He gave back what the enemy stole. Yes he did. Now fix your face and I'll see you in a bit.

The club was jumping the band was playing and the Second Line had begun. As she danced her way into the kitchen the staff stopped. Everyone could see there was something different she was different. Her dance was different and when the sound of the brass band paused, a scream from the depths of her soul emerged. And then as a perfect instrument the kitchen joined her in a celebration of liberty.

All right let's make this happen we have an hour before the first course. Mimi you and Tony appetizers. Allen drop those crabs and shrimp in the gumbo. Mia, I want those salads beautiful garnished with the lavender flowers. Jody meats and Mike your backup. Boo you and I will plate, time to rock and roll.

Ms. Ella came into the kitchen watching Honey as she moved. Honey Love what has happened? Honey did a shimmy and a shake, I'm free Miss Ella! God is good to me! She screamed the kitchen paused and everyone laughed. Ms. Ella started to cry with hands stretched to the heavens. I got it back Ms. Ella! Tonight, we celebrate your deliverance Honey Love Parquette! Now Ima dance as tears flowed from both women the two could only look up with raised hands. Child all this going on I almost forgot to tell you the Queens have arrived.

Ms. Ella left out the kitchen with a Holy Ghost dance. She informed the band to start the Doors of Grace theme song.

With fans and parasols in hand the Queens were ready to enter the building with a dance that's only done in Nu Awlins. The custom of the announcement always was followed by the entrance of Honey an honorary member.

Dressed in white shirts with a black and royal blue neck ties. Black pants and black patent leather shoes. The waiters took their place at the double doors of the kitchen. As the trumpet blew Honey came thru those doors with a new buck. Everyone could see something was different. She danced to the center of the dance floor and one by one dressed in red and white the Queens joined her. As Honey danced her way back into the kitchen, Gwen approached the mic. Heyyyy everybody welcome to the Doors of Grace! Tonight, I present to you The Uptown Queens and one by one she presented each one.

Back in the kitchen Honey never stopped dancing it was contagious the whole kitchen danced. Everyone was rocking and rolling. It was as if the Doors of Grace had been reborn. She was new. As the courses went out nothing but praise returned to the kitchen. What a night.

Leaving the club she turned and stood for a while, watching the neon lights from the sign sparkle on the river. Reminiscing on the days when she and Mademoiselle would sit and listen to the Mississippi as the riverboats gently pushed the waters. The lights flickered as they did on this night. Looking to the stars Honey began to pray. Oh, my Lord I thank you for one the best day of my grown life. Once again, your faithfulness has prevailed.

CHAPTER FIVE

The Queens

The Queens were more than a Social or Second Line Club. They were friends that always were sistas first. Becoming a club, well that was redemption.

It all started with Honey Love and Darlene "Red" Cortez. From being next door neighbors to kindergarten. They were always sistas. Maybe because they shared Momma hurt.

Red Momma got married and promised to come back for her. She never did and like Honey she had a grandma for a momma. And this is the pain they shared and the tears they swapped in time brought about a remarkable strength.

Red would work in the kitchen after school with me and Mademoiselle. She would tell us you never stop being taught. She taught us a lot.

On Sundays after church they'll rush home to meet the Second Line. And there in the dance was the escape from all that was wrong. It was freedom. The Queens begin with two lil girls determination to rise above all life circumstances. And as a queen rules her kingdom, so would they rule their lives.

In time the bond extended to those that was running from somebody or something. We all have something, Diana "Lil D" Brown lost her momma to pneumonia when she was thirteen. Pretty soon after, the man she had known her whole life as Daddy thought she should take her momma place.

She always found her way on top of some car. She would laugh and say, I have wings on my feet. She said it made her feel untouchable above life cares.

Leslie Dumaine, she ran to school. Any and every school that would allow her entrance. She was put up for adoption after being conceived through rape. And for a time she was passed from one family to another.

Finally she made it to Ms. Lyza and Big Daddy Thibodeaux. They never had children of their own. Ms. Lyza always took in those who parents for one reason or another couldn't handle it no longer. Sooner or later a relative would come and getem or they parents would come back when things got better.

The Thibodaux's got Leslie when she was seven and bitter.

Her insides were scared and ready to take on any Monster. But love is stronger than anything. Its true God knows what we need and even who we need.

Lisa Mixamus she had everything just right. Her daddy was the Deacon at Tell Jesus Missionary Baptist Church, her momma directed the choir. And when she sang she sanged. But living in Nu Awlins the music has a way of drawing your soul.

Midnight Blue, Blue said God had dried her tears away. And that was the reason she had no tears and no reason to cry. But instead all the reason to dance. She had to take care of her lil brothers Timmy and Johnny.

Ms. Blue was a real big singer, a star at one time. But stars sometimes fall and fall she did, becoming a dope fein. When the men wanted Midnight instead of her, she made the trade. But she was a slave to the dope. Her life was very public and when this happened everyone knew.

One night after praying Mademoiselle and Ms. Ella left the Doors of Graced, with a few men. They came back with Midnight and her brothers. She gave them the room over the club. She told her "You grown now, you can make a good life for yourself".

And she did, she owns the dance studio up on St. Charles Ave. Johnny became an electrician and Timmy a school teacher.

CHAPTER SIX

The Reunion

It's something about watching the sunrise, everything's clear. After a long night of darkness, you see a brandnew day. Old things are passed away, and all things have become new.

Hello. Hey Honey. Red, what time will we be leaving? I talked to everybody and we'll be ready to go at two. Who's driving? Gwen and Lisa. Blue said she got everything. Oh, and she talked to the chef at Babble Towers. And everything is taken care of. Honey you need to get to the café by onethirty. So, we can have a good prayer befo we hit this road. No problem, I'll be coming from the club. Ok see you later. Ok.

The day seemed to linger. Linger with excitement it was

the day Diana would be reunited with the Queens. We started arriving at Red's Café about one o'clock. Gwen and Blue was the first to arrive. The jukebox was playing the music that united a secrete bond. Coming in with ah dip and ah skip they formed a line. With a turn they did their dance the dance of the Queens.

Before the song had ended, they were joined by Lisa and Leslie. Heyy, heyy shouted Gwen. Today we dance! We dance the dance of freedom! And they all shouted heyy, heyy, heyy! When the song ended, they embraced one another. Being full of joy they all went into the office. Looking around Blue said. Sistas, I'm so excited this day has finally come. Don't cry Blue. Giving her a handkerchief, Red put her arms around her. Gwen proclaimed tears of joy! God has answered our prayers! With all in agreement the room became silent. Entering the office Honey began to pray…for the atmosphere was set.

O'Father God. It is you alone that have given us an unbreakable bond. Each one nodding while softly thanking Jesus. Lord we thank you for delivering us from the darkness of this world. We thank you that weeping endures for a night. Lord in the morning, in the morning comes joy. The joy of the Lord. The joy that is our strength. And this morning we all rejoice in unspeakable joy. Because this day you have set our Sista free.

We rejoice because it was you, that kept her safe these last five years. But more than that, we thank you for being

her judge. When the judge of this world said sixty years you said not so. Na Jesus, give us traveling grace as we get on this highway. And with one voice all said, amen. Standing their hand in hand looking up to heaven, their continence seemed to glow. Leslie said, He heard us.

Gwen said I have to tell yall something. This morning Connie came to the shop. For what Red quickly asked. She made an appointment, said her name was Emily. She was on time. You know I burnt Miss Callie hair. I just couldn't believe she was standing there. Taking a seat Lisa said. Gwendolyn what did she want? Well she said she knew Diana was being released and she wanted to wish her well. And she made peace with what happened. I asked her, is that why you lied your way up in here?

Red interrupting. She must think we forgot or don't know bout all those letters she been writing Lil D. The hell with Connie Brown! Do yall remember what happened after Lil D went to jail? Yeah said Blue, she told everybody she was gon kill D. Not only that the heifer got locked up. Honey spoke. Yep, and all yall went and got yourselves locked up. The room became silent then a burst of laughter.

Well that's why she said, this have nothing to do with the Sistas. I told her it always have something to do with the Sistas. And that she should have been trying to find some peace for Wayne. You was there when he pounded her face. Connie you know your brother was a no-good coward. You made excuses for his behavior. She said. Gwen you don't understand he was all I had. And I said, she is all we have. She started crying and said, I held my brother while he took his last breath.

I told her, I was there when her eyes opened after he closed them. Then I said, best thing for you to do Connie is leave my shop now. And stay far away from my Sista. If you don't. What happened the last time won't compare to what will happen. Blue asked did she say anything else? Say what? Blue there was nothing else to say. Do we have a problem? No, Miss Callie was all in the conversation. She said, she was moving back to St. Louis. Miss Helen told her she saw a moving truck. So, she asked her where she was moving to.

Well like I said. The hell with Connie Brown, and her excuse making self. Come on it's time to go. Everyone gathered their belongings and headed to the cars. The ride was full of stories. They reminisced on the good times as well as the bad. Now they were able to laugh at some things. Laugh because it's what a black woman does after sustaining a slap from life. Each one was an overcomer. They agreed that life disappointments didn't killem. Instead it created an unstoppable force.

Honey opened her bible and read Psalm 91 and began to pray. Pray about everything and for everybody. Prayed that the residue of prison life, fall off before Diana leaves the prison. And that her mind be released from the sorrows of the past.

They arrived at eleven-thirty waiting for midnight to open those gates. Waiting for her to walk through the gates

of life and death. Some call it "The Belly of the Beast". Blue shouted…I see her! Here she comes! Rushing to the gate with the excitement of children on Christmas morning. Watching it slowly open, Diana watched until it stopped. Standing there as if frozen.

Red went to her and said. Don't worry we got you. I know, I'm just so thankful for all yall. I know when I couldn't pray for myself, yall was praying. And now I stand here a free woman. Free only because the Lord gave me my time. (tears dropping) I love yall. I don't know what would have happened. If, if I didn't have yall.

Gwen interrupted, now we love you to. So dry dem eyes. Diana, you have a new life waiting on you. Your house is ready. All you have to do is decide where you wanna work. Get in the car D., you can take a last look at this place. Blue added…you will never see it again. Sista you got a good life waiting on you. Na come on let's go home. Walking to the cars arm in arm. As little children with hearts full of love. And an excitement loaded with plans of a bright future. Leslie has your door keys. Leslie handed her the keys. And Lisa said.

These are your car keys. Now let's go home.

CHAPTER SEVEN

Arriving home she noticed the extra-large bouquet of flowers. All her favorites orchids, gardenias and purple roses. Knowing who they were from she could only shake her head. Lord why have you brought him back? Help me Jesus. Tears began to drop as she picked up the vase. What am I going to do? Am I feeling emotions?

The sun crept thru the Victorian lace curtains, followed by an aroma that came from the kitchen. With the smell of bacon and chicory coffee her eyes slowly opened. Stepping into her slippers while putting on her robe she practiced what to say.

Standing face to face with Joey James Jones. Her absent husband the father of her child…emotions ran wild. Why did you keep the key? I knew I was gon come back. And why are you here Joey? I never stopped loving you Honey. But you left when you said you wouldn't. What in the hell do you want Joey?

Bae you wasn't the only one that lost a child. I was his father; I was supposed to protect him. Stop! Don't! You wasn't there I wasn't there. But evil was it was waiting on him Joey.

Have a cup of coffee, I made your favorite breakfast. Rolling her eyes, she sat down, all kinds of ungodly words rolled around her head. Honey sorry will never be enough. But Bae I truly missed you. Just stop! And don't call me that.

Joey, I woke up and you were gone. For the first time in eight years I woke up by myself. And you know what I did Joey? I got dressed, went to church and preached like never befo. The Monster took and killed my baby and my man left me. God was in full control. Jesus said He'll never leave me, and He never left me alone.

Honey please listen. No, you listen I am going to eat this lovely breakfast and drink my coffee. Then I'm going up those stairs pray and get dressed. Slowly stirring her coffee, have you seen your Momma? Yeah, she knew I was coming home. I made her promise not to say anything to you. When I called her to let her know when I'd be in town. She praised the Lord took a deep breath and cussed me out. Both kinda laughing. She thought maybe them folks got you.

Then the Lord gave her a dream. In the dream she heard a voice say, "Ethel look he's come home." She said she saw a jungle with beautiful birds and trees as far as you could see.

All kinds of animals. He told her she will touch your face again.

The Lord showed her, I went to Africa and that's when so much became clear. Stop. Joey, I don't want to do this with you. I'm glad a lion didn't eat you or no elephant stepped on you, like you did me. So, I'm just gon finish and we gon be real quiet. Honey Love I. I see a few knives left out, Honey Love what?

Now by time I do all these lil things I mentioned to you Joey. Well that should give you enough time to clean my kitchen and go anywhere. And don't forget to leave the key this time. Mmmm you always made the best lost bread just the way I like it.

Just then the doorbell ranged. Making her way to the door with plate in hand. Good morning Gwendolyn. Good morning Cousin. Breakfast at the door for me? No this is for me. You cooking early huh?

Joey is cooking early. What Joey? Joey James Jones? No other. What the hell? Yeah same thing I said. I have to get dressed.

Well, well, well Mr. Joey Jones what brought you back to Nu Awlins? Good morning Gwendolyn, how have you been? I've been good, the children are fine, all is well. Where have you been Joey? Why did you leave her? Coffee? Cream and sugar please…a lotta sugar. I traveled around, then I could no longer run from what I thought I was running from.

I went to Africa. Oooeee you Momma had a dream bout you in the jungles. She told everybody at bible study. Yeah her and her dreams. While I was in the Mother Land I found out, I was running from God. In church and running.

Gwen, I know this wasn't the first child Honey lost. You know? Yeah, I thought she didn't want children. Then one day she told me the fear of losing another baby. I left because I didn't know how to fix what was broken. Sooo do you know now?

All I know is I am more of a man of God then I ever thought I could be. I'm happy for you Joey James, boy give me a hug. You're still the same (smiling) I will be better to her than I've ever been. God will continue to show me how.

Hallelujah!

CHAPTER EIGHT

OUTTA THE DUGEON

So how is she really? It was hard for a long time but God kept her. She got her scream back. HALLELUJAH!

How? When? Recently and let me tell you she's been screaming. What a blessing.

Honey my blood Joey, and she's been through so much. I'm back and I'm back to stay. Mmm mmm well you better not stay today. All right Cousin. You got that look you had the first time yall bucked. She was like an angel. As I watched, look like her feet never touched the ground. Well that angel is running late so she'll be flying down them steps soon. You look good Joey I'm glad your back, it'll work out.

I dare him just show up leaving me flowers, using my key to come in my house. Cooking like nothing never happened.

Just acting like he wasn't gone one, two, three no I'm not going to count the years of my tears.

Now I can't find nothing to wear. Why did he leave me when he said he loved me? But I won't cry no I've cried enough about ah man. But this man!. Pushing back the tears, you never was supposed to make me cry.

Strengthen me Lord! I can't be thinking bout all this now, I got to drive to Pickallo. Jesus help me. Jesus I thank you, good thing you led me to Dr. Chester befo that man came back.

Help me forgive him. A part of me hates him for leaving when he did. But in my heart I still love him. Lord you said I have to forgive so please help me. Dry your eyes Honey Love Parquette. You are a Parquette, strong, capable, and unbreakable.

Lord you just gotta set me free today. I've carried my past with me much too long. I'm tired Lord, no more shame or guilt. What about Joey? She thought what if? What if things can be wonderful again. Putting her hat on and taking a long look in the mirror. Well I'll find out sooner or later.

This was the longest drive to Pickaloo, so many memories. Looking out the window she could see the cotton fields as far as she could see. Wishing she could see her life as clearly.

Good morning, I have a ten thirty appointment. Good morning Ms. Parquette the coffee is hot. No thank you. Your looking really happy this morning. Yes, Ma'am I got engaged. Congratulations I know the Lord will bless your union. Thank you, Ms. Honey, I mean. Interrupting shhh no harm done Bae.

The wait seemed endless anxiety took her hand. O'Lord Please not now I can hear my heart. Ms. Parquette you can come in. Good morning Ms. Parquette. Good morning Doc.

What is going on? Feeling anxious, angry, upset. My sons father showed up from nowhere! Your son? Yes, Joshua he was abducted some years ago. Tears streaming down her face. He handed her his handkerchief. I'm sorry for your lost. I hate when people say those words. Sorry don't compare but what else is it to say? Do you want to talk about it? No, that's not why I'm coming here.

What do you want to talk about? Right now, nothing, I shoulda canceled today. But you didn't. No, I didn't Dr. Chester my life has been one train wreck after another. And every time I think it's on track. BAM!

After a long silence she dabbed away the tears. Honey opened her pocketbook and slowly removed a gold cigarette case along with a monogram lighter.

I remember my debutant ball it was on my sixteenth birthday. I was so excited Mademoiselle had the most beautiful gown made for me. I even had special made shoes. She chuckled. It was at the Grand Ballroom of the Pontchartrain Towers.

It was the first time I did the Waltz. And my escort he was my brother. How many siblings do you have? I told you my Daddy was a musician, he toured more than some cities and clubs.

He had four other children I'm the third child. Only three of us live in Louisiana, me and Leon the oldest. The youngest Joseph, his momma married a service man and been living overseas.

Then its Anthony he's doing life in the penitentiary. I visit him often, a black man in the wrong place at the wrong time. Is there a possibility of him being released? I'm working on it.

It's me then Escot, he has his own company in New York. He's an architect. We visit each other four times a year and often talk.

And the last but the first is Leon the oldest. A stillness fills the room, looking out the window she whispered he was my escort. May I please have some water? I feel ah lil flush. Yes, of course. With trembling hands looking into the glass. Another skeleton coming out my closet.

I had only seen Leon a few times befo the ball. The first time we met my daddy and I went riding in his brand-new Cadillac convertible. (Smiling) I remember going across the river on that bridge. It was like I was so close to the sky. And looking down at the river, the sun made the dirty Mississippi look like floating diamonds.

Daddy said Honey I'm taking you to meet your big brother. I was seven, we are all ten months apart. When we finally got to his house, I knew who he was befo Daddy said it. He looked like the pictures of my Daddy when he was a boy.

After being there a short time Leon Momma came outside she was so mad. Boy, she cussed my Daddy from A to Z. He gave her some money and we left. I asked why she so mad? He said because I love your Momma.

The next time I saw Leon was my thirteenth birthday party. It was at the Doors of Grace. Stella, Leon Momma she came and made a lotta noise. Noise? Yeah fussing about how Leon was first born, and Mademoiselle made a difference and didn't keep Leon.

But nobody told my grandmother what to do. She had this gift she could look at somebody and know. Know if they were good or bad. Now she loved us all. But she said that Stella was no good. And her son Leon, had the same blood as his momma.

Why did she keep you? Because my Momma was special. Special how? She was church a good girl, who loved the wrong kinda man my Daddy. She couldn't handle his life. It was like she was light and in a way, he was her darkness. Her light gradually faded away.

Something bout the music it draws you. It brought them together. She was different than the women at the clubs. She was really church.

Believe it or not they met at church. She would go and hear him play.

One day she really looked around and reality hit. She wasn't the only woman there being serenade. He loved his music more than anything. Even when he wasn't playing that sax the music never stopped inside.

Long story short he married my Momma, she got pregnant and wala here I am. After I was born it all became way too much for her. At some point she moved away. Far away from my Daddy the music and me. Alaska imagine that. A cold silence entered the room.

The truth about her is she wanted to be the one and only. But that wasn't the kind of man he was. He use to say he loved her more than any woman. But he loved his music even more.

Looking out of the window she whispered he was my escort my brother. The debutant ball was on my sixteenth birthday. Sixteen was everything but sweet. I looked forward to that day the day of the ball.

Wiping the tears away Dr. Chester so much has happened to me. At times I feel as though I was destined for destruction, before I ever entered this world. Is that possible? But you were not destroyed. Yeah but I'm here. Why are you here? I'm tired of keeping secrets. You say secrets, do you have many secrets? Enough.

That night was like a fairy tale. My Daddy was there to present me. He was so handsome he was smooth as silk. I remember looking into his green eyes as he proudly and lovingly said, You look like your Momma. He loved her and she loved him but sometimes its not enough. That night changed something in him. I miss him and his music.

It started so perfect I mean truly a gran occasion. I had my brother it was a great feeling not being alone. After the ball was over everyone went to the Doors and it was a night like no other. Everyone was happy Leon and Daddy laughed, we danced, and we was a family for the first time.

It was getting late, so my Daddy gave my brother his car keys and told him to take me home. Leon make sure she get safely in the house. And then he was supposed to go back to the club and hang out with Daddy.

I was so happy I couldn't stop dancing. In the car, up the steps from one side of the porch to the other. I danced right in the front door. I thanked Leon for being my escort and how he made my day unforgettable. He said it will be a night I will always remember.

Then he began to look at me strangely. In a way a brother don't look at a sister. I asked him what's wrong Leon? He said ain't nothing wrong Honey Love.

I heard how you got your name Honey because you the sweetest thang in this ole world. Love I want to see if you as sweet as your name. Why you talking like that Leon? Leon Daddy's waiting on you. No, he's blowing that horn all he ever cared about is you and that damn sax.

I tried to run but he was faster and stronger. Like a lion that have found it prey. We fought my beautiful white gown was now stained with my blood and his. Ultimately he prevailed and I found myself in that tunnel again with the Boogie Man. (Weeping)

I was so confused and scared. He was my brother not a stranger. He ripped my dress off like a savage. He put a piece of the dress in my mouth. I was pinned down as if nailed to the floor.

He was touching me like a man touches a woman. I was a child his sister, but he didn't care. He penetrated me, took my virginity. I was supposed to give it to the man I loved. Sometimes I can still smell his skin.

When he was finish with me he got a warm towel. He then began to clean the blood off my face my thighs. It was like watching a movie I had no fight left only total confusion.

He was supposed to make sure I was safe. He was my blood but not my brother. Once again, the devil had me. But that time he actually got me.

When Mademoiselle came home, I could hear her screaming my name. She found me in the backyard I had to get out that house. I remember the look in her eyes when she dropped to her knees. Oh, Honey baby I'm so sorry. She cried out to God help Lord, help my baby. She said it over and over.

She wrapped me in her cape and thru her tears tried to tell me it will be all right. Momma got you Honey everything will be all right. But it wasn't I was not the same after that night.

I couldn't go back in the house so that night she put me in the car and drove to her best friend my Aunt Dahlia. I stayed with her for a while in that time my physical wounds had healed but not my spirit. After that I went to California to my other grandmother Pastor Pinkey Gray Ma Pink.

What happened to Leon did you report it? Report it? That's what

I'm doing now. I don't know what happened to Leon. But something happened to my Daddy that night changed him. He became broken, maybe it was guilt, shame when he looked at me. The looks were different they were sad even when he smiled his eyes said something else.

Did you and he talk about what happened? One day he asked the question was it Leon Parquette? And at that moment I began to apologize for what I don't know. That was the only time I saw him cry. He said, "Honey I'm so sorry please forgive me". I said Daddy he hurt me so bad. Why did he do that to me? He kept saying he was sorry. I told him it wasn't you it was Leon. He held me so tight and I was safe, he said he will never hurt you again.

Did he confront Leon? Leon just disappeared. They say he went to a gambling shack one night. No one ever saw or heard of him after that night. And that's all I know about Leon Parquette.

Closing her eyes with a deep breath she whispered I'm free. It's over.

CHAPTER NINE

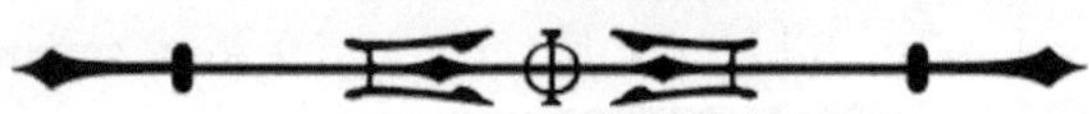

Bible Study

Lord get me through this bible study tonight. I better call Ms. Ella so she can be praying. Good evening Ms. Ella. Hey Bae is everything alright? Yes Ma'am, I need you to pray some walls down tonight. I've already started Honey. So just come on with a word for us. Ms. Ella had the Spirit of a Breaker. Her prayers could break down anything and anybody.

Good evening and to God be the glory. Tonight we're going to discuss unforgiveness versus forgiveness. I have been dealing with these for some years. I justify my unforgiveness with reasons to hold on to my reasons for my feelings. Well as we know there's always a scripture we use to try and justify our reasoning.

As Honey spoke the words began to penetrate the walls. Walls that were constructed to keep away anyone that betrayed or hurt her. But something was happening. Those walls began to come down.

As the words of her Lord pierced her soul. In her heart she begins to ask for forgiveness. So much gets buried in the heart. Allow Him to give you a heart transplant. Today our hearts and minds are clear.

Something began to happen in that room. As she cried out for the Lord's forgiveness it was like everyone had something or someone to forgive. And the belief that peace would replace the trauma.

After the study she and Gwen headed to the café. Gwen was like a pot of boiling water ready to discuss Mr. Jones. Girl I talked to Joey this morning and I heard what you said. Honey Love I know he hurt you. You had a double lost your son then your ole man. But it didn't destroy you, your stronger then you know Honey.

God has kept me my whole life Gwen. Before bible study I was dealing with me myself and I. But tonight I let go of me myself and I, I'm free Cousin. Praise the Lord, I'm happy for you. But what about Joey? I still love him. I never stopped wanting, needing and loving that man.

After we buried Joshua, we became strangers. We stayed busy to avoid each other. My baby was gone and there was no comfort. There was nothing he could do to fill that void. He had a void also it was his son too. You know I not only shut Joey out but God also for a while. Yeah I went through the motions, did church work and the daily day. All with a broken heart Gwen.

I havent heard you say anything bout, hum about. Sari? I always think about my baby. She will always be my baby forever.

Honey you thinking about Samson to? I think about how he loves me. It's a lot of pain but sometimes I do think of him.

You know Joey left me flowers again. That's Joey Jones. Calm down (shaking her head).

But now I understand, I was broken but not destroyed, left but not alone, confused but restored. Go head Honey Love Parquette. I must forgive him. I don't know what is going to happen with him and me. Well on that note let's order desert. Let's Ms. Gwendolyn Gray. (Laughing) it's good to see you laugh.

The next morning while doing inventory when Ms. Ella came in. Good morning Ms. Ella. Good morning my Honey Love. Bae, you seem so different. You're screaming your dancing like you on air. And last night was just amazing. You are happy ain't seen you like this in a very long time. What's going on?

I'm seeing a Doctor Ms. Ella. You sick oh Jesus help! No no, I started my medication again. This time I'm talking about things I've kept inside. It's time to let go and really let God. Hallelujah hallelujah give me a hug child. I'm so proud of you. Don't cry Ms. Ella. These here tears are tears of joy. Tell me about this doctor. His name is Dr. Lance Chester and he's in Pickaloo. Pickaloo, you go way to Pickaloo?

Yes, Ma'am I heard he was the best in Louisiana. I don't want the medicine. Ms. Ella, I prayed and the Lord sent me there. Well I know you're in the right place. Good for you Honey. Well tonight is the Unbreakables club night. The menu is on your desk. Thanks Ms. Ella. Finishing the inventory, she went to the French Market to pick up the ingredients. Strolling through the French Quarters her heart walked with Mademoiselle as usual. Remembering the stories about the joints my Daddy had his gigs at.

We would have lunch every Thursday where my momma and daddy would go. It was her way of letting me know they did love each other and me.

This is the love I longed for. A love in which I'm the woman he gives his love and heart to. To love me like my daddy loved his music. I saw how it took him to another place. He will look at me and see that I love and adore him. A love that would last thru eternity.

Standing in front of the Praline Shop, she thought I had this with Joey. After shopping she walked along the river, one of her favorite places.

Watching the Mississippi move as the riverboats went up and down the river. Gazing upon the water it began to dance to the medley played by a lonely musician.

Lord I want to be free, I gotta see Dr. Chester tomorrow. I have kept so much inside for so long it's time to let go. I have to tell what happened. It's time to release it all to you Lord. I now receive true happiness from you. Put me together Jesus.

Arriving home there was a bigger bouquet of her favorite flowers waiting for her. As she picked them up, something was familiar. The fragrance became that of Sari. The wind found favor and blew what was thought to be the forgotten scent of her daughter. Well this is a good night.

Hello Honey, can you pick me up today? No, not today. I'm seeing a doctor again. That's where you been going? Yeah. Are you taking medicine again? Yes, I just know, that after I've gotten all this stuff inside of my head out. Well then, I won't need the medicine. I'm proud of you Honey.

He's in Pickaloo the drive helps too. Gwen, I told him things I never told anyone. Not you, not the sisters, nobody.

I feel free. You look different Honey. I can see what freedom looks like. I guess so. I'm happy for you. You know Joey left me flowers again. That's Joey Jones. Calm down Cousin. The strangest thing when I smelled the flowers, I could smell the scent of Sari. I had forgotten how she smelled. But now I remember. Oh, Honey Love.

What are you going to do about Joey? Nothing right now, I'm working on myself now. God is answering my prayers. And the past is losing its hold on me. I don't know what's going to happen with me and him. But I do know I need to truly forgive him.

CHAPTER TEN

At Reds Café

Joey Jones is that you? Joey? Good morning Red, how you doing? Joey I'm good, everybody good everything all right. So, what wind blew you bac here? Have you seen Honey? Yes, I'm hoping to see her this morning.

I'm going to get us some coffee. Thank you, and I'm back for my marriage and my wife. Joey my Sista has come a long way, she can't take another heartache. I know you both lost Baby J, but hers was a double lost again. She told me you knew. Yeah and I see you still looking out for her. Always.

Red I'm home. The Lord has had his hand on me. I saw Ma Pink when I left Nu Awlins. She taught me how to listen, for that small still voice. How she doin? Still taking care folks huh? Yeah, she took care of me. She prayed me into my destiny. For the first time my eyes were open to the real things of God. I tell you the power that lil lady has is not of this world.

There was a lot of soul searching and just trying to make sense of what happened. The quilt I felt not being able to protect my son. Joey you wasn't there. Who would have thought somebody would go in a school and take a child. It was just one of those things no one saw coming.

The pain we felt. The hurt that closed the door, was written all over her face. I didn't truly trust God befo I left. But now, Ima watch God fix it. God got you Joey. And he got Honey Love. She never stopped loving you. And I love her more than ever.

Here she comes. Good morning Mrs. Jones. Good morning Darlene. I see you've been talking to Mr. Jones. Yes(smiling) he's back and he's different. Strolling to the booth arm in arm. Honey Love he say he saw Ma Pink when he left. So you know the Lord must have had something for him somewhere. Ok I love you Sista. I love you too. See ya later Joey.

Looking at her his heart whispered. Lord restore our love, give me back my wife. Give her a ear to hear me out. Hey Joey. I'm glad your morning routine haven't changed. No, I've been coming herein the morning ever since the first day she opened. Mademoiselle was so proud of Red when she opened this café.

Joey I can't stay I have somewhere to be. Well can you have a cup of coffee? A half of cup. I know Red gave you the third degree. No the second. O' Lord I know she gon be ringing the doorbell tonight. (Smiling) Why now Joey? I couldn't run nomo. I missed my better half. So, you just now missing your better half?

I missed you when I was here. Where did you go Joey? You don't know but I spent a lot of time with Ma Pink. She prayed with me and for me night and day. And then one night she woke me up about three in the morning. She said its time for you to trust God with everything. Pack your bags your leaving in the morning.

I asked her where? She said listen and you'll know. That's Ma Pink. Looking into his eyes she knew he wasn't the same man that left. She never told me you where there, but that's Pastor Pinkey.

Excuse me Joey I'll be right back. Watching her walk into the kitchen. Mmm mmm mmm. I love watching you walk. Suddenly this scream that caused everyone to pause. Returning to the table she smiled. It's time for me to go. It's time for me to go Mr. Jones.

Then she saw his tears. There was ah refreshing. With her handkerchief she gently wiped away his tears. Holding his face in her hands she whispered, I love you Joey James. I have to go but I'll talk to you soon.

The ride to Pickaloo was very different this time. This time the radio could not drown the thoughts and memories of the past. Hitting the brakes pulling over to the side of the road. She began to scream and cry. Crying for the children she can never again hold in her arms. Crying for the man she lost and the one that returned.

Dr. Chester arrived at the same time as she did. He could see she was distraught. After the exchange of greetings nothing else was said as they walked to the office.

What has happened Ms. Parquette? My husband has come back. Back from where? I guess from everywhere. California, Africa, London everywhere. Do you want to talk about it? No. Why the tears? Joey he's my second husband. And your first husband? We had a daughter Sari.

Doc after, well Leon. My daddy took me to Los Angeles to stay with my grandmother. I couldn't return to the house where I was so violated. My Daddy tried his best to make me feel better and assure me I was safe.

He had this look in his eyes, sadness. But we are Parquettes. Unbreakable able to overcome all this world could throw. But unprepared for what family can do.

My grandmother is a preacher, she left Nu Awlins following the Lord. And when my Momma went to Alaska, she went with her to make sure she was ok.

Mademoiselle said "Ain't nothing the devil can put on you that Pinkey Gray can't pray off." Fear had a hold on me, and confusion was my bed partner.

My Daddy stayed a couple of weeks playing in the jazz clubs put there. His music had become sad, like me.

I went to school and in the evening, I helped out in the kitchen. I thought she was a preacher. She is, the Lord told her to go to California. And there was a lady she was to pray for. You know when she got there from the train she went straight to her front door.

They had made room for her. But she would go down to the east side and pray for people. Feed them if they were hungry. She'll go to jails and visit people she didn't even know. She always said the Lord got your name and number?

After Ms. Martha got healed, who she went to Los Angeles to pray for. She and her husband gave her their home. A mansion with land and everything in the house. With a smile, they said the Lord told them to give it to her. That's amazing muffled Dr. Chester.

The house is in what's called Sweet Mountain. When entertainers came to the city they would stay at her home. She says Gods people deserve the best. She always ministered to them. It is a kinda church for those some believed to be Sinners.

Is this when you got married the first time? Yes, to Samson Malone he was my true love. We had a daughter Sari. I lost them both at the exact moment in time. Handing her his handkerchief she gently dabbed the tears away.

Ms. Parquette your shaking, maybe you should sit down. Doc I haven't talked about Samson or Sari in years. But the pain in my heart is like an old broken bone on a cloudy day. You don't see the rain, but you know it's coming.

She sat down and removed her shoes. Picked up her pocketbook and once again removed the gold cigarette case and lighter. Do you smoke? No, I don't, it was my Daddy's, sometimes a girl just wants her daddy close.

My wedding is the first and only memory I have of my parents together with me. How do you feel about that? Feel. I accept my relationship with them both for just giving me life. My Daddy is and has always been here for me.

My momma, I've come to understand we can't always play the hand we have been dealt. My grandmothers always reminded me of her love for me. I pray for her because I know what its like trying to capture and hold thoughts at bay. And they never told me anything but the truth.

She loved my daddy without a doubt, and it was just too much and with me. I vaguely remember her. How old were you when she left? After my fourth birthday you see I have some helluva birthdays.

On my wedding day she gave me a pair of diamond earrings. As she was putting them on Daddy came in, and we all just kinda froze. No one really knew what to say but her eyes said it all. Hello Charity. Hello Baron. Your as pretty as you were on our wedding day. You and Mademoiselle did good with our girl.

Your beautiful Honey. Thank you, Daddy. I just wanted to let you know even though your soon to be a married lady. Well, I'll always be there if you need me. Look at you all grown up. I love you Daddy. As he held her in his arms, she thought this is the last time he'll hold is lil girl. All right now don't cry. Baby girl, this is just the beginning of the happiness you deserve.

Charity how long will you be staying? Baron can you give me a moment with our daughter. Sure, sure I still love ya Charity. I know and I will always love you Baron Parquette. Good seeing you. Take care of yourself Baron.

At that moment I understood I came from a sweetness that he tasted. And a love that will last throughout eternity.

Oh no, no mo tears my Love. That man has a way of making you cry, laugh, and fly on a cloud all at the same time. While touching up Honeys makeup she said. We both love you very much I need you to know this. I love you more than you will ever know.

Momma do you really still love. Yes. I do and your Daddy was like magic so full of excitement we traveled we prayed. And then you came Honey Love our life was perfect you completed us. Enough of that. You got a husband waiting on you.

Love did find me. Yes, and it always will. Mademoiselle said he's a good man. And she's never wrong seeing the good and the evil in somebody. Momma thank you for coming. I love you my baby.

CHAPTER ELEVEN

Healing Love

Samson was kind and a musician. He played the piano at church. He had a band that played at his daddy club, the Last Step. Ma Pink stepped in there one night after praying with a drunk that had just left the club.

She said the Lord led her into that juke joint and right to Mr. Malone. He shut the place down. And that night he got religion and so did Samson.

Did you talk to your grandmother about Leon? Yeah, we talked about everything. I just didn't tell her the things he did. Why? She already knew, she saw it in a dream the night it happened. She said she woke up praying for my mind. I was happy in California but as my life goes it didn't last.

The church was getn ready for the annual beach picnic. The entire community went. That was the one day, when folks ate all that was Nu Awlins. Pastor Pinkey was a great cook. She is the kinda preacher who understands, people needed a balance. Dr. Chester have you ever seen the ocean? Yes I have, a few years ago.

The picnic was my first time. I thought, I can really not be found in this water. Just lost forever. Not like the river at all. Just a body of water as far as you could see. Being there near the water made me homesick. And sick to think about going back home.

I found this huge rock, the waves hit the rock. I felt The coldness of the water on my skin. It felt like my heart.

In the middle of my daydream, I heard this voice. Why do you look so sad? Why you by yourself Miss Honey? Hey Samson, just thinking about the Mississippi. That muddy water? Yep. Then he just sit next to me not saying anything but saying so much.

I had been seeing him for months at church he was always polite. And never more than good morning or good evening and whatever church business we had to discuss. And in time I began to see him seeing me.

I remember looking into his brown eyes and wondering, are you like my daddy? Will I be like my momma overwhelmed, overpowered by the thing called love. And I was I was finally able to see the love Mademoiselle wanted me to see that my parents had.

Pretty soon the pain that brought me to the west slowly faded. For the first time I loved a boy it felt so good it was right. And yet my soul longed for the dance the music and my Grand knew it.

It was a Friday night when she surprised me, she had a hifi and my daddy records. We danced half the night. And after our fingers were blistered from popping, we sat Indian style on the floor.

Taking my face in her hands she said, "It's all in the Master plan. Your life will be a life of joy and pain. Ups and downs, happiness and sorrow. Trust the plan of God Honey Love".

It was a Thursday night Samson came by the house after getting permission from my Ma Pink he took me to his daddy joint. I had never been there before, but it felt good being there. He handed me his pocket handkerchief and walked over to his piano sung me a melody he called it "My Honey Love". It was beautiful he knew how to keep me smiling.

I have ah surprise for you Miss Honey. His band began to play Second Line music. As soon as I hear those horns my feet began to move, and it was like I was floating. I hadn't danced since the night of my debutant ball my birthday.

Samson knew the mashed potatoes, funky chicken wasn't the dance I needed to do. But the dance we dance to celebrate life and death. And I danced life back into me that night.

Six months later we were married. I can hear his words so clearly. Marry me Miss Honey and I will be there emotionally mentally and spiritually. And he was he was all I needed, and life became great.

The wedding was beautiful all my Sistas were there half of Nu

Awlins seemed like they were there. My daddy had a smile that had been erased had returned. We were all very happy.

Our wedding night was magical. Standing at the threshold of our future, I took a deep breath. My heart begin to pound, as my mind raced back to that awful night. The tears swole up in my eyes. Samson held me close and tight. He held me in his heart. And slowly the beat of his heart became the beat of mine.

Love me Honey, and I will be here for you. I got ya emotionally, spiritually, and physically. I will never hurt you Honey Love. I'm gon love you cause I see you. I know you love me. Trust me Baby. Lifting her chin, he wiped away the tears that fell one by one.

And after my first kiss. He carried me to the bed. I started to tremble. Samson quickly assured me I was safe. Fear shall not destroy my love for my husband. Fear will not rob me of the love he has for me.

Don't worry Baby everything is all right. Taking my hand, he slowly walked me into the bedroom. He sat me down and removed my shoes. Walked around to the other side of the bed. As he took off his shoes and started to sing. I loved to hear him sing sometimes he wouldn't talk, he'll just sing. I understood. Tonight, is the beginning of a lifetime. Looking at his kindness and tenderness at what was so messed up in me.

Samson Malone, I love you and I need you to. He whispered in my hear. Your perfect. I kissed him and it was sweet. He tasted like a sweet summer fruit. And I wanted the whole fruit, not just a taste. We made love for three days. (smiling) We ate and bathed. He was magic everything a girl could want. I loved Samson with every fiber of my being. Like magic the fear left and that night.

I taught Sunday school and young adult bible study. Samson he could sing like an angel. People would shout until they were loose from whatever brought them thru dem doors.

Life was perfect but as my life goes it came to a perfect end. One Friday night Samson was at the Last Step playing that piano. I understood the music and the life that went with it. But unlike my Daddy he only had eyes for me.

Did you go to hear him play? I went once a month. Why once a month? It was our arrangement, besides we had a piano at home. He played and sung the most beautiful songs. Pretty lil girl just about blew my mind, that's what he sung to Sari and me.

That Friday night started off as any other day. He made grits and fish for breakfast and we were off to our business.

Me and the baby spent our days at the mansion seeing to the guest. It was always somebody there.

Sari was fussy that whole day crying more than ever. I thought she was teething, but it was much more than teeth coming. So much more than I could imagine.

Midnight, it was midnight when there was baming on the door. It was Curtis, Samson brother covered in blood. He didn't have to say anything. I grabbed the baby and we prayed all the way to the hospital.

Everyone was waiting on me he was waiting. He got shot, a fight broke out and so did the guns. They say bullets were flying and two hit my husband.

I put my hand on his face and laid our daughter on his chest. Miss Honey Ima love you for eternity. And then (crying) with one breath he was gone I picked up my baby and she was gone too. They both was gone I wanted to die. Once again, my world was shattered. I buried them together she was in his arms.

The doctors say they couldn't explain why her little heart just stop beating. But the marvel of it all at the same presice time as though it was one heart Samson and Sari was gone.

After that Daddy felt it was time for me to go home. Honey its been a long time since you went with me on the road. At this point it really didn't matter where I was, I could not be with my love or my child. But he knew the one place circumstance and situations would lose me. Where was that?

In a kitchen a different kitchen. We traveled for a year it was like every other joint had a kitchen. And I was welcomed to accompany his music with my food. The best part of the excursion was Memphis.

When we got there, he said I have a surprise for you my Honey Love. I'm determined to see your eyes dance again. Ain't no words for the things that have happened to you. The Lord has you on a journey that started from a child. And one day it will be clear. We praying for you and I see prayer working, you smiling again.

When you was born yo Momma said you will always have love. Samson last words to you was, he will always love you. He took his love for you into eternity, that's always. And Sari, she completed that family you missed out on with me and your Momma. Never doubt her love for you Honey, that woman loved you more you will ever know.

Pulling in front of the Grandmaster Hotel. This is where me and yo Momma stayed every time we came to Memphis. With a puzzle look on her face every time? She traveled with me all the time (with a grin) she was my girl.

Extending his arm, he said I'm going to tell you about me and yo Momma. You never talk about her. I truly loved her Honey with all my heart. Nobody could hold a candle to Charity Gray, and she knew it. After checking in we went into the bar. Watching him as he looked into that glass it was as if he stepped back into time. This look I never saw before. A smile a man as when he looks at is woman knowing she's his.

Charity stole me from Connie Green. Ms. Green? Yep, Ms. Green (laughing). Foreal Momma actually stole you? Yeah, she stole my heart. It was on Juneteenth it was a big picnic on the lake. She use to catch me looking at her in church, oh she was so beautiful. But more than beauty she was full of life. I became a rich man from the music I made playing bout her. I didn't know that.

And so, we at the picnic the band playing and yo Momma was dancing down. You dance like her. I was sitting there with Connie. Charity second lined her way to me. she looked right pass Connie. Looked me in my eyes and said.

I see you always watching me Baron. From this day on I'm your girlfriend. My Momma? Yes, yo Momma. And she was my girlfriend until she became my wife.

Its almost supper time you better go on and get ready. I'm gon take you to where we performed together. This is like a dream. But it was all real. I can't wait, you know you my hero. You have always known what to say or what to do. Thank you for being here Daddy. We got eight o'clock reservation. We can walk from here.

Strolling down Blues Boulevard was more like Memory Lane. The excitement in his voice as he reminiscence of the good times they shared together and as a family.

Arriving at the Keyhole Supper Club, we were met at the door by Moonshine Davis. He got his name Moonshine from selling moonshine. That's how the he open the Keyhole.

Is that Baron Parquette the smoothest sax player on this side of the Mississippi? Moonshine, how you been man?

They embraced and shared a couple of private jokes. I was really sorry to hear about Samson and the baby. Thank you, Mr. Davis. You sho look like your Momma. She would bring the house down her and yo Daddy. Charity favorite table was right over there and tonight its yours.

Moonshine motioned for Elaine the waitress. Hello Baron. How you been Bae? Great. Will you be playing tonight? No we just having dinner and a night out. Ok if you follow me I'll take you to your table. Elaine, can you direct me to the ladies room? Sure, follow me.

Returning to the table she couldn't sit fast enough before asking. Daddy why you never told me about you and Momma befo. Probably because I felt like I made her sick. She was a good church girl and I didn't know how to fix it. And maybe I just had to save it for now. We was good together Honey she still have my heart.

During dinner he told many stories of places they went the times she would sing with him. She was my spotlight. But she kept the spotlight on Jesus. She would have a prayer meeting wherever we went. And the Lord answered every prayer she prayed for somebody. Like Ma Pink? That's where she got it from. The fruit don't fall far from the tree.

Doc that night revived me, it gave me a sense of who I was. But more than that I got to see her thru his eyes. To know her personality the time she spent with me.

Quietly strolling back to the hotel, the snow began to fall. We stood there I felt the coldness upon my face. And once again the comfort of the all Mighty shadowed me. It was as though heaven filled all the little holes in my heart in my life.

With my hands lifted I said. Daddy the Lord has answered my prayers and the pain is not there. God has given me a new heart. Hallelujah Lord I thank you for my life and all that you have carried me thru. Thank you, Jesus, for a father and mother that loved me.

Watching his daughter praise, he knew that she was going to give life another chance. Going in her pocketbook she took her handkerchief and wiping tears from both their eyes said, let's go home Daddy. Ok baby girl were going home.

What happened when you got home? I was all right for a while, but the thoughts and memories overwhelmed me. I tried suicide again. What was your method that time? Pills, my cousin Gwen found me. She was determined not to let me die. And now no matter how I try to shake the thoughts I can't, I'm like my Momma.

No, Ms. Parquette what your mother experienced was depression after having you. The changes to her body her life, her ability to cope with the responsibility of caring for a little human. Along with the reality of your father life- style all became over whelming to her.

Doctors understand it better, but there's still much more to find out. Cutting his words short. Why ah mother don't love her child. Sadly, but yes. Doc this is what finally broke me and made me realize my momma blood runs deep in me.

Like Leon our blood was tainted.

I've lost a lot my children, love, and time. But the good Lord has been kind to me. He did send me someone to love me. My second husband Joey James Jones.

Do you smoke? No, they belonged to my Daddy and sometimes I just need to hold onto these. But Doc its time for me to go. I'm going to give you something to take. Ah happy pill? I hope so, you're going to take one at bedtime. Okay.

I'm glad I came to Pickaloo, and you should come by the Doors of Grace as my guest and bring a guest. Well thank you, I'll do that. Will I see you next week? No, I'm free now. I feel it in my heart the pain is gone. The broken pieces of my life has kept me sad in the inside for so long. But today a realization that all what happened and didn't happen did not destroy me. Thank you, Dr. Chester.

As she walked to her car in her newfound freedom. Life became new, she was new. Leaving Pickaloo she pondered on what she would say to Joey. But all she wanted was for him to hold her in his arms. To feel his heartbeat next to hers. To hear him say I love you.

Oh Lord thank you for bringing him back and not taking his love away. And now Jesus I'm going to see my husband ignite our love as in the beginning. Teach me how to truly love this man the new man you sent to me.

I need to let him know his wife misses him. Stopping at a phone booth. Hello Joey. Hello Love. I need to see you today. Is everything all right? Yeah, Joey better than it's ever been. I'm on my way back to the city and we need to talk. Ok Bae. Joey I'm sorry for not being there. No need to apologize all that matters is now. I love you Honey Love Jones. See you soon.

CHAPTER TWELVE

Lost and Found Love

Would you like to get some dinner? Yeah, I would. Love there's so much I want to tell you. How long have you been back Joey? Four days ago, it was late when I got in. But the next day I left you flowers. And the next day you made me breakfast. I want to take care of you, I've grown up.

You still fine Joey James. I love to see you smile Love. Just as they were about to pull off. Bishop and First Lady Moore was driving by. When the Bishop saw Joey, he hit the brakes so hard it knocked his hat off.

Bishop Bishop. Joey Jones, you made it back. Sorry I haven't called yet. Oh no worries, glad to see you called your wife. Me and the wife was on our way to dinner. You and Honey should join us we can catch up.

The Bishop would like for us to join them for dinner.

Bishop More was that uncle that wasn't a real uncle. But was one of the men that would step up in a boy's life when they daddy wasn't around. It's like they say it takes a village to raise a child.

When Joey left, he left Bishop Moore in charge of his parking lot business. Joey daddy had two lots he passed down. And in time two turned into seven. Joey and Bishop Moore had a special relationship a father and son.

When I left, I went to Los Angeles and I stayed with Ma Pink. When I tell you she is a praying woman! Yeah Pastor Pinkey, I hear she's doing great things in that city. Honey (whispering) Teedy she never told me he was there. Na Honey Love, you know when it comes to the things of the Lord, she ain't talking to nobody but the Lord.

We listen as though spelled bound to each experience he had. He had even learned some of the languages. But more than that he had an encounter with the Holy Ghost.

Who is this man she asked herself? I've never seen Joey like this before, never heard him like this. Lord he's different a new man. It was like meeting him for the first time. I want my husband, maybe we're both fixed, maybe the mercy of God has fixed us. Her hands began to shake. Lady Dalilah slowly and gently took her hands. She whispered breathe and with a smile and a wink that anxiety left. But she knew my heart she knew my life. And as always, her presence brought peace and this feeling of protection.

Arriving at the Queen Ann's Riverboat. I think they almost forgot us in the back seat. Lady Dalilah said, Bae we'll be in directly. Ok Darln. Get a table I'll find yall. Well let me help you out this back seat. Thank you, my Baby.

Teedie you something else. Yes, I am(laughing) and like you I got a husband who I make smile all the time. I see how that boy look at you the same way he did when he first started coming around. Not long after you came back from California.

I was a mess. But you're not now and he loves you baby. I know you scared. But do you trust God? Of course. Well if that's true see the love the Lord has sent. I know you love him. Yep I do. Ok so let's not keep those gentlemen waiting. Give me a hug lil girl. Thank you.

The evening was a blessing. It helped us get pass the awkwardness of getting to know each other. A lot can happen in three years you die or grow, I did both. As he talked of his travels and his time of self-observation. And once again I asked myself who is this man. The Lord had blessed him with the power of healing, and many were healed in the revivals he attended.

The Bishop told him he wanted him to bring the message on Sunday. He was so excited about the way God had been using him. A refreshing rested on Joey. Looking at him she couldn't help but wonder. Can I forgive me for pushing him away. Yes, Honey Love that is what you did.

Bishop and First left after dinner. We stayed listening to the music.

Reminiscing on how the music brought them together. Mardi Gras day the music summoned him into the Doors of Grace. Joey was the president of Gentlemen of Leisure Soul Steppers. Boy you know we was a match made on the dance floor. The night was going well.

(Strolling along the riverbank). Joey, knew it was a place that brought her a peace that calmed her nerves.

Joey I'm sorry for not being there for you. No, you don't have to be I understand you had lost two children. I never blamed you Love. It was something we would have never been prepared for. No, we wasn't. Do you remember that morning? Yeah, Joshua woke up laughing. He had a dream he was flying in a rocket he went to the moon. You never told me that, but I remember how happy he was. He said he was in the stairs in his rocket. Joey, my baby didn't know he would be leaving this world. Please don't cry Bae.

Joey why did that man pick our son? Why him? I can't answer that, he was just evil. Do you think he suffered much? I know my baby had to be terrified. Crying uncontrollable Joey held her as she began to fall to the ground. He picked her up and carried her to a nearby bench.

Honey Love it wasn't the beating that took our son. It was his heart. His heart? You didn't want to talk about any of it. I didn't tell you because it was the same as Sari. OH MY GOD! What's with me Joey? My babies, what have I done?

Oh Lord no what is wrong with me? Joey, Joey I miss them so much. My babies will always be my babies.

Honey Love, it's nothing wrong with you. Bae it was the divine hand of God. Joshua's heart just stopped. Love, he was gone before most his injuries. (Sobbing) Hold me Joey hold me tight. Hold me Joey. I got you Love, baby I got you.

Let's go home. I'm here Honey Love and until death do us part. I'm here Baby.

www.ingramcontent.com/pod-product-compliance
Lightning Source LLC
Chambersburg PA
CBHW051236210726
48290CB00003B/987